# LOKI'S DIGITAL D

BY

TANYA WHITE

Copyright © Tanya White, 2023

The right of Tanya White to be identified as the Author of the Work has been asserted by her in accordance with the Copyright, Designs and Patents Act 1988

All rights reserved. No part of this publication may be reproduced, stored in a retrieval system, or transmitted, in any form or by any means without the prior written permission of the author, nor be otherwise circulated in any form of binding or cover other than that in which it is published and without a similar condition being imposed on the subsequent purchaser.

All characters in this publication are fictitious and any resemblance to real persons, living or dead is purely coincidental.

"The world is full of magic things, patiently waiting for our senses to grow sharper"

(W. B. Yeats)


"There are things known, and there are things unknown, and in between them are the doors of perception"

(Aldous Huxley)


"All that we see or seem is but a dream within a dream"

(Edgar Allan Poe)

"We are all in the gutter, but some of us are looking at the stars"


(Oscar Wilde)

Biography

Tanya White is a human rights barrister, practising from Ventnor. She is the acclaimed author of a number of previous books, 'The Thirty-Year Night', 'Re-Setting the World', 'Olive Trees in Norway' and 'Loki's Game of Cards', as well as 'Feelan the Monster' and 'Santa Needs a Little Help' for children.

She has three children and two grandchildren, and now lives on the Isle of Wight with her husband and their Old English Sheepdog, Basil.

Accompany the Bottomleys on their hilarious voyage of uninvited discovery of reality and fantasy.

Does our diet of fake news, misleading profiles and manipulation alter our perceptions of what is real? To what extent is our reality distorted? What does it take to pierce that distortion?

The answers lie in your own perceptions.

# LOKI'S DIGITAL DYNAMITE

| | |
|---|---|
| Chapter 1 | Infiltration |
| Chapter 2 | The Party |
| Chapter 3 | The Plan |
| Chapter 4 | The Action |
| Chapter 5 | Supply and Demand |
| Chapter 6 | Ephemeral |
| Chapter 7 | The Enigma |
| Chapter 8 | Eros |
| Chapter 9 | Digital Illusion |
| Chapter 10 | Cyber Crime |
| Chapter 11 | Chaos |
| Chapter 12 | Divine Intervention |
| Chapter 13 | The Search |
| Chapter 14 | Above and Beyond |
| Chapter 15 | The Gifts |

| | |
|---|---|
| Chapter 16 | The Levington Solution |
| Chapter 17 | The Coup |
| Chapter 18 | Disaster or Great Fortune |
| Chapter 19 | Reality and Perception |

# LOKI'S DIGITAL DYNAMITE

by

TANYA WHITE

Chapter 1.

INFILTRATION

As the thunder roared and lightning struck the earth Mother Nature was furious.

The Bottomleys were terrified, shaking, tense, angry, matching Mother Earth in fury. The next terrible event could happen at any moment. Gerry was halfway through her spreadsheet. Rodney was doing his tax return, at the 11$^{th}$ hour. Josh was at the pitch of his gaming. Jenny was competing on Twitter. Phoebe was nearly at the end of her computer puzzle. They all knew, at any moment, the perils of cause and effect, yes, the weather could interfere with the internet connection!

Conversely, Gunnhilda was so bored by the digital world that she felt enslaved. It was not time, but she begged her father, Loki, "I must come back now. This world is so dull. All day they are at screens. I want to fly among the clouds, sail across the oceans, scale the mountain tops, breathe in freedom, release my spirit...please, Father."

"Come on, Gunny, there's great sport here. Infiltrate their digital world and you can have fun, fun, fun. Now what's the best cure when you're a bit down? You know. I've just been playing with the Chinese digital spy implant...a little tweak here and there and that's just for starters. Go shopping. Buy whatever you want. Your funds are currently endless!"

Feeling much better, Gunnhilda amused herself sampling the joys of Fortnums, Gucci, Harvey Nichols...

"Guys, come on, look, I've bought you all some presents. Here, Jenny, a silk embroidered gown for your party. What's wrong?"

"I'm sorry, but that's not what we wear."

"Why, it's beautiful?"

"None of the influencers dress like that, nor do my mates. We wear this sort of thing…here, on my computer."

"But why would you wear clothes that have rips and holes?"

"Because everyone else does."

"Why?"

"Influences, fashion."

"So how do you become one of these…influencers?"

Gunnhilda's gifts were rejected, but she did get a crash course in the current mores of the young.

"Geraldine, how on earth can Gunnhilda afford to give these expensive gifts?"

"Not sure, Rodders. You don't suppose...?"

"What, Gerry?"

"Shoplifting. I mean, why work as a nanny if she doesn't need the money?"

"Because she loves her work, wants to do something, to make a difference."

Gerry wasn't satisfied, but let it go.

## Chapter 2

## THE PARTY

Jenny had just arrived, coat still on…shocked, she quickly turned back.

"Dad, wait."

"What's wrong?"

"OMG! I can't go in dressed like this. Got to go home and change. Dad, they're all wearing these long dresses. Cheap imitation silk, mind, but I'm off kilter. I don't understand."

She saw the latest influencer, saw the likes, referred to her friends. She shuddered.

"Dad, I'm out of the loop. Gunnhilda was right. I hope she hasn't returned that dress. I won't be able to go to the party if she has."

"Look, Jen, is it actually you who's been invited to this party, or is it your clothes?"

"Not the point Dad...please."

# Chapter 3

## THE PLAN

"Mum, it's not fair. Julia's got an amazing bedroom. It's been designed by Lois Harvard Franklin, she's got a four-poster, Barbie wallpaper, glass sliding wardrobes, wool carpet…"

"Jenny, it sounds hideous. Anyway, we don't want to be sucked into consumerism, it destroys the planet, it becomes addictive, it wastes your time."

"Mum, I'm not asking for all that, just a decent makeover. Flowery wallpaper is so yesterday, and that wardrobe I had when I was 6 years old."

"If we do your room, we'll have to do Phoebe's and Josh's. It's unnecessary and time-consuming."

"What if I pay for it myself?"

Josh smirked. "You haven't got any money."

"Jenny"

"Yes, Gunnhilda?"

"I can give you money."

Before Gerry could protest, Jenny got angry.

"No, I don't want your money, or Mum's, I'm going to get a job at the weekends. I'll do it myself."

Gunnhilda protested. "Jenny, give me a day or so before you commit to anything. I just need to get something approved at the Council offices."

"You'll need a year to sort out anything at the Council. What do you have in mind?"

"Leave it to me, Geraldine. Have I ever let this family down?"

Yet again, Gerry let it go.

"Good morning, may I help you?"

"Yes please. My name is Gunnhilda Lokisdottir. I am here on urgent business. I need a licence for a market stall forthwith."

"So sorry, you will need to apply, in triplicate, on the net. Go to the Council's website, at this address" handing Gunnhilda a printed slip "and once you have done that you will be assigned a password and given further instructions. You can log back in about 6 months' time, and you will then…"

"Let me see your manager, now."

"I don't like your tone, Ms Lokisdottir."

"Leonard Brightspark, manager here, how can I help?"

By this time Loki had successfully hacked in.

"You will see on your system that my application was approved over a year ago, but I haven't received the licence. My solicitors will be issuing a claim for damages for loss of earnings without further reference to you, if I don't have my licence forthwith."

"Goodness me. You are right. Ms Beaver should have checked this. I do apologize."

Gunnhilda had her licence forthwith.

"It's a lovely idea, Gunnhilda, but probably a waste of time."

"No, Rodney, trust me, the kids will have fun and earn money."

"Sorry, but no-one is going to buy groceries from a market stall at a higher cost than they would in the supermarket."

"Please, I've ordered and paid for the perishable goods now, and I have the licence."

"We're happy to try it out" said Jenny and Josh together.

Chapter 4

THE ACTION

Willowfield Supermarket was particularly busy, even for a Saturday. Each till had long queues, both the manned and the self-service ones.

"Gunnhilda, we've been here an hour and had no customers. Dad was right."

"Wait another 30 minutes, you'll see."

"Shit, what's happened?" asked Miriam on one of the tills. "Bevan, get the manager, quick."

"I can't see him. All the bloody computers are out, and the tills won't work. Hang on, there's Mr Ponso now on the tannoy."

"I am sorry to announce that our computer system is currently down. Our tills are in consequence unable to work. Unfortunately, this means we are unable to complete any sales, and I must ask you to leave your shopping and vacate the store. Our engineers are working urgently on the computer system now, and as soon as it is fixed, we look forward to welcoming you back. Thank you for your patience."

The customers were furious.

"I've sent 2 hours in here getting my shopping and now I have to leave it all."

"Yeah, hope the bloody ice cream melts."

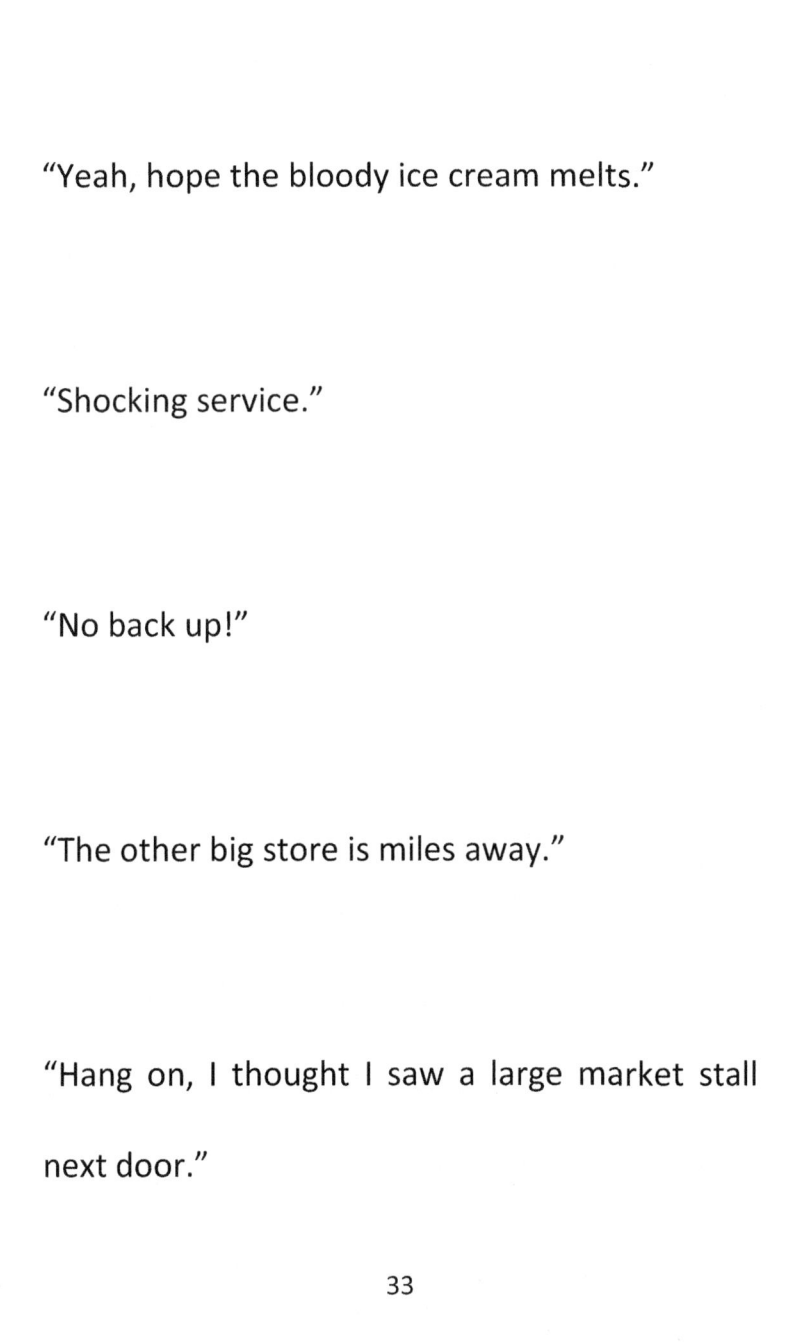

"Shocking service."

"No back up!"

"The other big store is miles away."

"Hang on, I thought I saw a large market stall next door."

They all rolled out, hustling and bustling, and eventually queuing.

"There will have to be a limit on your quantities. Even then we shall run out." Gunnhilda engineered at least a semblance of civilised behaviour amongst the hitherto irate customers.

"These prices are quadruple the price in Willowfield."

"Please don't buy them, other customers will. It's a question of supply and demand." Gunnhilda was having fun.

They returned home exhausted and shared out their profits equally, giving little Phoebe Gunnhilda's share.

"Got any more ideas, Gunnhilda?"

"You bet, Gerry."

Chapter 5

SUPPLY AND DEMAND

The Chancellor of the Exchequer, Gayleaf, chaired the inter-ministerial crisis meeting. Solemnly he began. "As you are aware, the impact of global warming has caused the destruction of swathes of crops. We cannot import so much now, and a bottle of olive oil, for instance, is now more expensive than a bottle of Chanel No 5. You will see from my report that the International Monetary Fund and the Bank of England are singing from the same hymn sheet. Interest rates must double, post-haste, lest inflation drowns us all. The data is on page 251 and in appendices 4-400, which have the actuarial figures. I have, as you know, the PM's agreement, albeit reluctant, to press ahead. Your approval will assist in getting the public to swallow it. Yes, Mr Sirius?"

"This will not do. You cannot suddenly double mortgage and other interest rates overnight.

People haven't had time to budget. The cause and effect scenario will outweigh any attempt at inflation control. House prices will plummet. Businesses will go under. This is ridiculous."

In unison "Hear hear".

"The alternative is worse" Gayleaf continued. "We'll end up like Germany in the 1920s, needing a sack of money for a loaf of bread. I am sorry, the mandate is in motion, and it goes to press as we speak. You can all help or hinder. Yes, Mr Blacklake?"

"We are being bullied. This is grossly improper."

"As has been said, hard times call for hard measures."

There were a lot of very drunk ministers that evening.

## Chapter 6

EPHEMERAL

"Rodney, we'll have to sell the house. Our outgoings are already overwhelming us. I can't believe it, doubling interest rates overnight!"

"Yes, I agree. The kids will have to change schools, and I suppose the nanny will have to go. We'll have to manage. Phoebe is at least at infant school now."

"No, Rodders, Gunnhilda stays."

"What? I thought you always seemed to resent her somehow."

"She's grown on me. So wonderful with the kids. Remember how she saw off that gang of thugs bullying Josh?"

"Oh yeah" he laughed "putting that transparent cord across the entrance to the school sheds, getting Josh to stand there, they came charging at full speed and all fell, very undignified. I thought the manure under the leaves was over the top, but still…and then removing the cord unnoticed, and when Josh proclaimed 'Higher powers' they all believed him!"

"Yes, exactly, Rodders. She's wonderful with their homework, everything."

"I know, darling, but we just can't…"

Gunnhilda had been eavesdropping. She seized the moment. "Hello, sorry, I'm not interrupting am I? I don't think I ever mentioned this but, excuse the pun, I have friends in high places. Even as we speak plans are in motion to alleviate this current economic crisis, but it is on a 'need to know' basis only. Just give it 24 hours before you take any drastic action."

"Rodders, I don't think we'd be doing anything that quickly, would we?"

"Oh no, Gerry. But Gunnhilda, what is this all about?"

"Confidential, sorry. Must fly."

As the ministers met for their 4th crisis meeting in the basement under the Cabinet Office Loki, god of mischief, Foresti, god of justice and Caishen, god of money met in much higher quarters for their first crisis meeting.

"Look, Foresti, I know we don't aways get on, but surely you can help out here, with all those poor souls going bankrupt, losing everything?"

Caishen intervened. "Yes, and for nothing. I tell you, money in their world is crazy. So much is intangible, ephemeral, digital, with big bucks hanging around in the ether. And as Loki knows, you can just play with it like a toy. You probably saw the collapse of the latest digital currency, called Dodo! Disappeared in a puff of smoke, leaving all those supposed billionaires as real paupers."

Foresti reluctantly bought in to the idea. Caishen took up the running. "I will liaise with my digital infiltrators. It's relatively simple to hack into anything in the digital world, certainly for us. It already contains our viral sleepers, Foresti, don't worry. There's little difference between their intangible money 'in the bank' and their digital money in the ether. It's just about how they perceive it and their confidence, or lack of it, following on. It's about

being bumped around by different events."

Chapter 7

THE ENIGMA

It was a post-graduate economics student at Cambridge University who first spotted the anomaly. Gladys Minelli was working into the small hours, late with her thesis. She was shocked, freaked and also elated. She started talking to herself, wishing she hadn't taken those bloody uppers. "Is this true, or is it alcohol plus Ritalin plus no sleep? I can't wake the Professor at 3am, can I? But this is mega."

Professor Mozeley was startled by the apparition. Was he dreaming? A beautiful young woman with flowing dark hair and a voluptuous body entering his bedroom uninvited at 3.05am. Was this a gift from the gods? In a way it was, but not in the way he thought.

"Professor, please, set up your computer to this web address." But she could see he was in shock. "Never mind, I'll do it…wait…read this data…NOW!"

"Good God, you break into my room and make demands at this hour?", but after further begging and pleading, and some serious twitching on his part, he turned to the screen and read.

It was 5am on Sunday, 8h October 2025. There was a crisis meeting in the PM's office.

"Gayleaf, how has this happened? Are you sure about this?"

"PM, we have checked and re-checked. All the top people are in unison. The inflation figures were completely wrong and the monetary fund is swimming, not drowning. As to how this happened, we suspect cybercrime, aimed at destabilising our country, causing unrest and economic decline, to set in motion a falling tower. As we speak the Intelligence Services are working on the case."

"Rodders, have you seen the papers? Look, I bought 6 different ones, just in case."

The Times: - Inflation normal. Government sources say they are considering the possibility of a cyber attack aimed at destabilising the country by infiltrating the Government's financial data systems.

The Guardian: - Total irresponsibility of Government ministers, failing to confirm their data before setting in motion an economic snowball.

The Independent: - Thousands suing HMG for shock, pain and suffering, and reduced monetary sales, as a result of its negligence in failing accurately to assess its own data.

The Daily Mail: - Communists infiltrate the financial world in bid to destabilize the country.

The Morning Star: - Western economy sends out fake news, to make the rich richer and destroy the working man.

The Mirror: - Chinese hack into digital dynamite!

"Gunnhilda was right, but how did she know?"

"I don't care right now Gerry, I'm just bloody relieved."

Chapter 8

EROS

"More coffee, Gerry?"

"Oh, yes…erm…I was thinking, it is a bit odd, Gunnhilda predicting so much, settling so much…I wonder if we should…no…let it go."

"No. I've been letting too many Gunnhilda enigmas just go. It's time we investigated her background. Maybe a private detective?"

"That sounds a bit sneaky, weasel-like. How about something quieter, say a little personal foray on the net? Oh, gosh, hi Gunnhilda, didn't hear you come in. There's coffee in the pot, still hot."

"No thank you. I'm off for a few days tomorrow, need to sort out a few things. Have you arranged cover, is it still convenient?"

"Oh yes, of course."

Gunnhilda wondered whether she shouldn't just come clean. They would find nothing out of the ordinary on the net, that had long been sorted. They would remain totally confused. But then she remembered what had happened to Njord. Ironical, she thought, here he was, god of the wind and sea, and of prosperity, and look what happened. He fell foul of Eros and disclosed his true origins to a mortal, Jasmine, having fallen in love with her. Oh yes, he broke the covenant, badly, and was punished. He was banished to Iceland, to exist eternally on a diet of frozen food. Still, she wondered, what happened to Remus, the son of Njord and Jasmine? She busied herself on the internet and began typing.

"Hello Remus. You don't know me, but our fathers were once great friends. I think it sad that yours was the victim of Eros' arow. I heard that Eros had made a mistake (it is said due to intoxication). Well, once released, cause and effect was set in motion, your father had no choice. Foresti put up a good case for him, you know. But the consensus was that it would set a precedent, so Iceland it was. So sad. How he hated that food.

Anyway, I hear you're in London meeting the Ambassador about civil rights. If you have any free time, can we meet?

Gunnhilda."


One hour later… "Hi, Gunnhilda. You intrigue me. I presume your digital profile is totally misleading, much like mine. I admire the way you fathom the depths of one's soul and apply the practicalities of simplicity to find me out. I'm a misfit in both worlds. My friends are not real, and my dear mother has died. I work hard to distract myself, but loneliness is my middle name. The Old Black Horse in Spitalfields at 7pm. See you then. We'll just now each other. If we don't, it wasn't meant to be."


7pm... "Gunnhilda, you are just as my dreams dictated. You are beautiful."

"Remus, you have your father's fine stature and transfixing violet eyes."

"Ouch!", in unison.

They hadn't realised, but Eros was drunk again, arrow in the wrong place.

"Come, Gunnhilda, let's fly above the clouds, let's dive into the seas, brushed by the winds."

"The sea is warm, Remus."

"No, it is we who are warmed by the electric sparks of love and passion, shaken in a whirlwind. Look over there, Gunnhilda. Let's rest in that cave for a while, come, let me hold you."

Meanwhile Zeus had summoned Eros.

"I have spoken with Odin. It seems you have once again been negligent and have damaged the normal order of cause and effect."

"Well, I'm sorry, but do understand. There's no harm in the end. In fact it often works well for détente. I mean, that mistake with the Russian President and the US President's daughter actually improved relations."

"Don't give me that, Eros. More often than not it caused chaos. Remember the Catholic priest and the Buddhist yoga teacher? The rabbi and the girl from the triads? The mullah and the First Lady? That scientist and his robot? Oh no, this has gone too far. Now you'll have to remove the arrow from Loki's daughter and Remus."

"That's really hard work."

"Well you've done it many times. All those divorces. Get to work, and then report back and we'll see what we shall do with you."

"You need me. No world can cope without love."

"Insolence! Out!"

Gunnhilda started to look at Remus in a new light, and he too…

"Er…I don't know what to say…my feelings, Remus…I mean…you will always be a dear friend…er…"

"It's okay, Gunnhilda. I feel the same. Maybe this really was a whirlwind romance."

Chapter 9

DIGITAL ILLUSION

"Good evening, Gunnhilda. Did you have a good break?"

"Oh yes. I sailed the high seas with a soulmate, scanned the depths of the sea with our very souls, got caught in a whirlwind and scanned the skies..."

"Ha ha." Geraldine and Rodney thought she was joking.

It appeared that normality reigned in the Bottomley household. Everyone was glued to a screen. Curious, Gunnhilda decided to "screendrop". She would start with Jenny. She busied herself with some embroidery, as a front for some mirror espionage, and there it was. Jenny was on a dating app. Gunnhilda scrutinised the profile. This was no boy of 16. She read their exchange.

"Don't worry, Graham, I'll tell Dad I'm staying at Lola's, I've done that for her, she owes me. See you at the Tiger Club, 9pm tonight, remember your white rose."

"See you then, gorgeous."

Gunnhilda was beside herself. If she revealed all this to Geraldine Jenny would be devastated and would never trust her again.

"Jenny, Josh, dinner's ready."

"Coming Mum."

"Gunnhilda."

"Thanks Gerry, but I've already eaten, just catching up on some reading."

As Jenny left the room, Gunnhilda hacked in. "Hi again, can't do 9pm, tell you why later, can we go a bit earlier, say 7.45pm?"

"Sure darling, see you soon."

Gunnhilda swung by the Ulysses Fancy Dress Emporium, then on to the Tiger Club, going straight to the Ladies. Locking herself in the cubicle, the transformation began.

George had spent hours trying to make himself look 10 years younger. It hadn't worked. Excited, eager, he was like a predatory animal, hackles up, when… "Who the hell are you?"

"I'm Jenny."

"What? You're a bloody freak. Your skin is grey, you're wearing a purple wig, you must be 5 stone overweight, and how much make-up are you wearing?"

Gunnhilda was relieved that the fat suit worked – it had cost a fortune. She smiled, showing yellow and black teeth, courtesy of well-applied dental cosmetics.

"If you're discriminating on the grounds of how I look I'll report you."

"You don't look like your bloody picture."

"Well, you don't either." She pushed his toupee, revealing greying hair.

George stormed out.

Back in the cubicle, Gunnhilda transformed again. She now sported a rough grey beard, the same dental display, scarred grey skin, dirty nails garnished with a hint of yellow fungus, and the odd boil for completeness. She, now he, ordered a whisky, though only for show. She couldn't risk drinking it with her dental display. On cue at 9pm, in walked Jenny.

"Hi, my lovely." Gunnhilda's acting skills exceeded even her expectations.

"You're nothing like your picture. You're a pervert, I'm reporting you to the dating app."

"Jenny, I thought you said you'd be staying with Lola tonight?"

"I know, Mum. We had a bit of a falling out. It's okay, but…"

"Do you want to talk about it?"

"No...er...thanks."

The dating agency in fact received two complaints. They were perplexed.

Chapter 10

CYBER CRIME

Odin and Zeus summoned the gods. "We know that what will happen is not of your making. This they did themselves. Nonetheless, we must intervene, or we will lose our sport. Caishen, it is, I believe, your flock, you must lead."

"Mum, there's a beep alert on my mobile."

"Yes, we all have one."

3pm. Prime Minister's emergency address.

"The intelligence services have alerted us to a criminal cyber infiltration from hostile parties. Our experts have been working around the clock to address this, and are confident of defeating it, but as a matter of precaution and until the system is fully secure the Government is asking you to take the following steps. Please obtain emergency supplies of battery radios battery lights, candles and non-perishable foodstuffs, along with bottled water for emergency supplies. Return to and remain in your homes. The transport system cannot presently be relied upon. The Government has allotted funds to suppliers for these essentials to be distributed on a pro rata rationed basis. Please listen for further updates."

Chapter 11

CHAOS

Geraldine came back flustered.

"I've got the basic supplies. What on earth is all that stuff, Gunnhilda?"

"A generator, a large battery radio, a water tank, large battery standard lamps and some extra food supplies."

"What are we going to do without a computer or TV or Alexa?"

"I bought these as well, Jenny."

"What are they?"

"A manual pottery maker, a vintage typewriter, an accordion, two guitars, a chess set, some puzzles and paints…"

"Doesn't sound too bad" Josh piped up.

"Is it okay, Gerry?"

"Oh yes, thank you, very wholesome. Why not share?"

Gunnhilda left to round up some of the neighbouring families, who were still all hoping it wouldn't come to this.

"Mum, look, that plane."

"What? Oh my god, Jenny, yes, it's flying backwards!"

"Computer's gone."

"Quick, Rodders, turn on the generator."

"The computer has power, Gerry, but it doesn't work."

"Rodders, the traffic is at a standstill."

The Bottomleys settled down with their neighbours. There were cards, chess, sewing, painting and a veritable smorgasbord of vintage activity, which kept them all surprisingly absorbed.

"Hey, Jenny, this is odd."

"What, Julia?"

"I've got a spare joker."

They let it pass.

"Good morning everyone. Come on, you must have finished breakfast by now."

"What's the point of hurrying, Gunnhilda?"

"Jenny, look outside. It's a beautiful day. How about we all go foraging in that enchanted wood?"

"Well, I suppose there's nothing else to do."

"Over there is a thousand-year-old oak tree."

"How do you know?"

"Josh, bring your friends over, I'll show you. See those circular lines, the rings on that stump. You count them and that tells you the age of the tree. Then compare the size of that stump and the size of this living tree. You can see it's bigger, with more layers of growth, so it's older."

"What's that great gungy fungus?"

"It's just that, but this is a fungus that grows only in unpolluted places."

"I can smell garlic, Gunnhilda."

"Yes. Sorry, what's your name?"

"Julia."

"This is wild garlic. We'll gather some and make a pesto, that will brighten up that tinned stuff.

We'll cook on an open fire. Now, how do you distinguish edible from poisonous mushrooms? Oh quick, there's a red squirrel. And there's a pheasant."

"Gerry, the kids seem to be adapting with aplomb to the situation."

"Actually, Rodders, I'd forgotten what fun nature could be. I feel free – obviously worried, but, well, in the moment free."

"Absolutely. And the bees and birds don't fly backwards because of a digital hitch!" they both laughed.

"Jenny, I've just lost that spare joker."

"You probably just imagined it, Julia. Come on."

Chapter 12

DIVINE INTERVENTION

"This is not a joke, Prime Minister. We cannot fathom how our systems have been infiltrated, or how all communication outside the country has stalled. We have been blocked by many of our allies for fear of contamination."

"For heaven's sake, Riceling, you may be my Personal Private Secretary, but you're no judge of character. If I didn't laugh, I'd cry. Everything, utilities, supplies, finances, is digital, the back-up is bloody digital, so it's all failed. Ledgers went out with the Ark, along with manual skills. The digital world is our world. If that has gone, we'll sink into anarchy. Even the police can't keep order without technology now. I can't send in the troops, they can't move a finger without technology. We need a bloody miracle."

"Rodders, look here, my phone's making a funny noise, it's going fuzzy."

"Mine too, Gerry."

"Hang on, what's going on with the TV and computer screens?"

"Quick, everyone. What the hell? Who's that man?"

"His name is Loki, Rodney"

"How on earth do you know that, Gunnhilda?"

She remained silent. The whole family, their friends and neighbours, felt a sense of awe as they glued themselves to the screen. After some fuzz and buzzing a handsome, distinguished-looking man had appeared. He had dark hair, sculptured features, high cheek bones and a slim build. He had a tattoo on his hand; it was a joker. In a deep, resonant, almost mesmerising voice, with perfect poise and diction, he began.

"Soon you will all be reunited with your greatest love…the digital world. It appears to have engulfed you, desensitised you, stupefied you, gnawed away at your sense of awe. It appears that you have invested everything in these digits, basing everything, both essential and non-essential, n their realm. In so doing, you left your cards open to ridicule. Your digital god has no loyalty, no honour. It is a tart, open to anyone who can enter. So obviously it had to happen, an infiltration spreading through the digital veins, causing a haemorrhage of untold violence throughout your society.

So what happens when it all breaks down? Always you ignore the beauty of nature, the depth of real, personal emotional contact, the beasts of the earth and birds of the air, and all these other gifts from the Gods. But when you invent a false world and exist within it, coming crashing back to real earth you cannot cope, so you pray for help and hope for a miracle. This takes work on our part, it is not fun, you are not sporting. Still, we have done what we can. Soon you will be back on line, back into your unreal world. But a warning. Much data will be lost for eternity. We, even we, cannot fully fathom the depths of digital data. But there you are."

"Mum, Dad, look!"

"Shush, Josh."

"But Dad, he looks like he's disintegrating...and now transforming. His tattoo, look, it's getting bigger...it's like being on magic mushrooms."

"How do you know what it's like being on magic mushrooms?"

"Just something I read, Dad."

Chapter 13

THE SEARCH

"I'm sorry, PM. We cannot identify this man, and it's not just us who've been working on that. His majesty wants to find him to give him a knighthood. According to MI5 the Russians, the French, the Americans and various other governments, plus the Triads and other organised criminals, are all actively looking for this ephemeral genius. But so far, nothing. It's like he disappeared into thin air, after first materialising from it."

"Riceling, are you suggesting that this man is some sort of apparition? Are we to consider some sort of supernatural, hocus pocus twaddle? Or is he a clairvoyant, if you please? Look, Riceling, I don't care what you do, just find him. We've got to retrieve the lost data. Hell, we've no records of mortgages, loans, savings…"

"But PM, he says he can't do this."

"Of course he can. We'll offer him eye-watering remuneration, all the help he needs, whatever. If our enemies get to him first, God knows what could happen. Get me Commissioner Wilcox, and General Smythe.

At Scotland Yard a conference call was set up. "Good morning, Prime Minister," said the Commissioner. "You will see that we are being joined today by Assistant Commissioner

Richardson, in charge of Special Branch, who will take the lead in the search, and also by a senior officer from the SAS, whose help we may need to enlist. There will be a lot of legwork on this one, as well as more modern intelligence gathering; old style meets new, as it were. All leave has been cancelled and unlimited overtime will be available. For once we are not constrained by a budget. I have asked Chief Superintendent Simkins to organise a newsflash and appeal. We should get a lot of information, Prime Minister. Someone must have come up against this man. His appearance is certainly distinctive."

The newsflash went out for the first showing while the meeting was in progress.

"Gerry, we can't let this go anymore. Gunnhilda called him Loki. Where is she? We need to contact Scotland Yard."

"She's out in the woods with the kids, Rodders."

"Doing what? Their screens have been back on for some time."

"I know. She said the call of the wild had entered their souls."

"What does that mean, Gerry?"

"Jenny and her friends said that the fresh air and exercise had made their acne disappear and it was fun. Josh and his mates wanted to climb trees, forage for food, chop wood and make open fires and generally align with light and nature. Oh yes, Josh wants fishing gear for his birthday and Gunnhilda said she would teach him. And Jenny wants a microscope and biology kit."

Hi Mum. Brought some mates back. We're starving."

"Josh, where's Jenny?"

"Here I am. Julia's staying for tea."

Gunnhilda came in carrying the fruits of their foraging and began preparing a wild feast, with a horde of hungry teenagers playing sous-chef. Geraldine put the microwave ready meals back in the fridge.

After the children had eaten, "Gunnhilda, may we have a private word? You may not have heard, you've been foraging all day, but an appeal has gone out for anyone who knows anything about this man. The are calling him "the Genius" but you know his name is Loki.

Please come with us to the Police Station and tell them everything you know about him."

"Good evening, madam. May I call you Gunnhilda? I'm Superintendent Penelope Marlington. I understand that you may have some information about 'the Genius'".

"Well, he's my father. That's why I'm called Gunnhilda Lokisdottir. He was born about 4,000BCE. He's the Norse God of Mischief. He got involved in this on the orders of Zeus and Odin – I imagine you know who they are – and has been assisting Foresti, Norse God of Justice and Caishen, Chinese God of money. Now, he…"

"Sorry to interrupt, but, um, thank you so much, that has been so helpful. It's very good of you to come in and give us this help, but that will be all. PC Froggit will show you out."

"Any joy, Super? The team are waiting."

"No, Franks, she's a complete nutter, it was a waste of time. Get Social Services to assess her.

She needs help. And phone those Bottomleys. I think she's a nanny, and she shouldn't be anywhere near kids."

"Gunnhilda, you're back quickly. What happened?"

"They didn't believe me Gerry."

"What did you tell them?"

On hearing Gunnhilda's explanation Geraldine and Rodney poured themselves a stiff G & T, just without the T.

"Gerry, can you get the phone?"

"Hello, this is Amanda from Merryland Social Services. May we have a chat?"

"Gunnhilda, can you give us a moment please?"

"Gerry, she's insane. We shouldn't have her as a nanny."

"I know, but the kids will be devastated."

Gunnhilda overheard all this. Knowing that she was dangerously close to breaking the Norse Code of the Gods, she seized an opportunity.

"Excuse me for interrupting, but my family are in a crisis and I must return. I'm so sorry. Tomorrow I shall explain everything to the children and will leave them three gifts. They will understand."


Relieved, Geraldine and Rodney made polite noises, hugged Gunnhilda, and then topped up their Gs (still no T!)

## Chapter 14

### ABOVE AND BEYOND

Gunnhilda metamorphosised into her true nature, a free spirit, shaken from the minutiae of earthly chains. She skimmed the ocean, straddled the clouds, spun round the moon, transformed her atoms beyond the cosmos into a formation that was her true self. She was free. She was home.

"Yes, my daughter, it was time. We might have played a little longer, but I fear too much attachment might backfire. Foresti is now working with them, obviously under the eyes of Zeus and Odin. It is no longer my toy. But you may have erred in leaving those gifts."

"But Father, the children would have been devastated otherwise. I had to leave them some comfort and that could only arise through understanding. Anyway, they wouldn't say anything lest they get subjected to psychotherapy and given labels. They know what happened to me."

"Still, my dear daughter, you stepped too deeply into the emotional arena. You were taught the perils of this, the impact on your reason, the inability to let go. As Eros has told you, true love means being able to give and stand back, to set free with confidence and without control."

Back in the Cabinet the PM was reining in his emotions with a heavy dose of mood stabilisers, prescribed of course, but washed down with Armagnac, not prescribed.

"Give me the figures Rupert…IN SUMMARY!"

The Chancellor handed over the report.

"What does this mean, Rupert?"

"Well, in a nutshell, as you know, our capitalist system works a bit like a turning wheel. It is normal for the economy to go and down, and around. With confidence the market goes up. It will, proportionately and in accordance with external influences, either crash or leap and then return to some sort of stability, with the help of the odd tax tweak here and there. But if it were to leak (though at some stage soon it will become obvious) that we have no back-up data for mortgages, pension funds, credit loans savings and other important things, then, if you turn to page 500 of the report you will see..."

"Are you saying that the country will be bankrupt?"

"Worse actually. The entire capitalist system will fold. We would have to seek international help, and how we would do that I don't know. They haven't responded favourably so far, they have blocked us, apparently in fear that their computer systems will be infected by whatever plague has hit ours. Or we would have to revert to a system of rationing all resources and hoping for the best."

"Are you suggesting we go back to the bloody feudal system?"

"Not exactly. But Lord Godfrey Levington, leader of the British Communist Party, may have to be brought in to advise on the restructuring of the British economic system. It could be worse. Godfrey was one of us once. He was in the same house with me at Eton. Fine rower, if I remember correctly."

"I know. What changed him?"

The PM's personal assistant, Raymond Fortescue, piped up.

"He used to go the same gentleman's club as me, in Chancery Lane. He was never comfortable with his status. He used to say that eating oysters in black tie while people begged in the street didn't feel right. That bee in his bonnet started making rich honey with the global warming crisis. He reckoned the answer lay in redistribution of resources. He also felt that the UK should lead the way and all that. He was firmly of the view that the Russians didn't have real communism. They were too controlled and utilitarian. They needed a more human approach. He used to say that Jesus was a communist, quoted the Bible a lot, stories like sharing the loaves and fishes to feed the 5,000, or the command to sell all one's goods and follow him. PM, are you okay? You look rather red…ah, excuse the pun, inappropriate remark!"

Rupert jumped in. "PM, I think we're going to have to raid the war chest, and get Levington on board. Remember, he's got a considerable network of clandestine moneyed contacts. We cannot rely on finding the Genius, and even if we do, we cannot be sure that he can magic up the lost data."

Chapter 15

THE GIFTS

The children sat together in Josh's room, music up and computers running. Phoebe was mesmerised. "I'm going to show Mummy. Look, this is beautiful."

"You can't. It's all secret. No-one will understand."

"But Jenny, we share everything with Mum and Dad, don't we?"

The elder siblings laughed, then, solemnly Jenny made the decision. "Look, guys, Phoebe's right, just for the wrong reasons. We know Loki must be traced. We might be in trouble if we keep schtum. These gifts are not just orange amber, they hold the abstract image of Gunnhilda, some atoms of hers are with us, that's what she said. We can reach her somehow, not sure how, but…"

"Darling, this is all very interesting, but…"

"Mum, it's true."

"Yes, Jenny, I know you all believe this, but, well, there's no image in these stones, just possibly some insect remains."

"No Mum, we…"

After much discussion, protestation, indignation and disbelief, Geraldine and Rodney felt the children needed help.

"Thank you, Hattie, it's kind of you to assist with counselling. I am afraid this nanny has somehow brainwashed the children. We are very concerned about this obsession."

"No problem, Gerry. In fact, Superintendent Marlington had alerted Social Services and the school is on notice. There's no cause for alarm.

Having had input from both sources we have designed a 6-week programme of counselling, mostly out of school hours, so it shouldn't affect their schoolwork."

"Thank you again, Hattie."

"What you and Rodney need to do is gently steer them through the illogicality of their imaginings, the scientific impossibility of leaving 'oneself', abstract or otherwise, in a stone, for instance."

It didn't work, at least from Rodney and Geraldine's end.

"But Mum, people believe that Jesus walked on water and rose from the dead. They believe Shadrach, Meshach and Abednego walked and talked in a fiery furnace. They believe Moses parted the Red Sea.

"That's different, Jenny."

"Well, different people perceive different phenomena."

"Josh, what are you on about?"

"Well, Dad, some people see names in colours. Some see people's auras. And when you're on magic mushrooms I'm told you see a whole different world. Who's to say that's not real?"

"Not those mushrooms again! Josh, where are you getting this stuff? Is it that bloody nanny, foraging in the woods?"

"No, no Dad."

Geraldine and Rodney took time out. "It's ironic, Gerry, but I'm almost relieved."

"Why?"

"Obvious, isn't it? They're taking magic mushrooms, drug testing, that's what we need. Far better that than getting them labelled as vulnerable, or prone to psychosis or whatever."

Chapter 16

## THE LEVINGTON SOLUTION

Godfrey Levington was hallway through his steak tartare, sipping a Chateau Haut Brion, in his country residence with a group of his closest friends. Tchaikovsky was playing in the background and the group were engrossed in a discussion of Marxist philosophy when the phone rang. Levington was minded to ignore the interruption but Angus, the butler, insisted.

"It's Raymond, my Lord."

"What can I do for you, Rayster?"

"You've heard the news? Well, that's not the half of it. MI5, MI6 and Scotland Yard have absolutely no leads in trying to find this chap called the Genius, and also apparently known as Loki. There are loads of fakes, but nothing real. Our intelligence services also reveal that the same dead ends are affecting other services like the CIA, as well as people like the Mafia, the Triads and other organised gangs. Oh yes, we've got men in all sorts of places, something you would have known if you'd joined the right party instead of playing Lord Lenin."

"If you want my help, Rayster, you're whistling out of tune. Now, what is it?"

"Unlikely, not even sanctioned by the PM, but worst-case scenario, we may need to reorganise the political, social and economic landscape. The thing is..."

"What? No bloody data back-up? All washed up in the clouds? Money in the ether?"

"We need a fall-back strategy, and you have it."

"Cometh the hour, cometh the man. Consider me pissing out of your tent now, Rayster."

The PM wasn't sure whether having Levington on board was a relief or a nightmare. He made this clear in Cabinet.

"My mandate from the British people was to uphold the free market economy, the kinder face of capitalism. You'll have to modify your ideology, Levington, meet somewhere in the middle, or people will revolt.

"With the greatest of respect, PM, current statistics, at least those just prior to the data loss, show 50% of the population below the poverty line, to varying degrees, I grant you, 40% not far above the poverty line, 9% considered reasonably cushioned and 1% super-rich. Please don't smirk, Rupy, yes, I was in the 1%. But no more, thanks to your incompetence. But I see this as a blessing in disguise...about bloody time to practice what I preach.

Now, I've sounded out a number of contacts – favours owed, a few promissory knighthoods, pre-approved UK citizenship and so forth. The transfer of intangible money is impossible, given that we are considered computer lepers by the international community, currently blocked from the global internet and in digital isolation. I hadn't thought that was possible, until the West did it to Russia over Ukraine. Anyway, the finance will be a mixture of gold bullion and cash. Don't worry, I've organised transport and security."

"What security"

"For some shipments, mercenaries loyal to me, and for some the SAS, PM. We shall then enact central control, with redistribution of wealth and sweeping nationalisation. Most people will find they are better off so they won't be complaining. The other 10% can protest as much as they want – it's a free country and all that – sorry, Rupert, you wanted to say something?"

"I have organised a PR mission, headed by Gloria Mountbatten, so the public are fully versed in what is happening here. I believe she will be using Levington's labour incentives…returning to manufacturing, more farming, no reliance on imports…"

# Chapter 17

## THE COUP

"I shall convene a crisis Cabinet meeting at 5pm tomorrow. You will have my decision then."

"PM, we all need to agree on this."

"I know, Rupert, one step...Oh yes, ask Barbara to tell Frieda I won't be home tonight, sleeping in the Parliament rest room, and, er, the usual supplies."

"Sure, PM, but I cannot guarantee Frieda won't intrude in the early hours. Your wife is a force to be reckoned with."

So true. 7am, Frieda marched into the PM's private space, physically and mentally, a force far greater than any of the gods could ever master.

"Bruce, what's going on?"

After a night of insomnia, the PM stirred from deep slumber. Opening one eye, he saw a large, burly apparition, fuzzy thick dark hair, bright red lipstick, 80s style suit, long false red fingernails, eyes glistening…

"Oh, er, good morning, Frieda. What are you doing here?"

"Never mind, what have you been thinking? A half-empty bottle of Scotch, ashtray full of cigar butts, chocolate wrappers? What kind of weak-minded man are you, needing props when the chips are down?"

"Er…well…chips are down Frieda, in more ways than one."

"Who are you phoning?"

The PM whispered "Get security, Rupert, asap! Sorry Frieda, I can't fight you and the Cabinet."

"I have made my decision. We are the manifestation of free enterprise. We were put here because of this. Our people have chosen conservative policies. To turn suddenly completely opposite to all we believe in must be wrong. I will not, cannot, be a red leader. Oh, must you interrupt Rupert?"

"Sorry PM, but the Cabinet is unanimous. The whole landscape has changed. Conservatism rests on confidence. Take that away and you have a house built on straw. We believe people can and will adapt. We have devised a programme of explanation."

Heated discussions bore no fruit, serving only to raise the PM's blood pressure, making his skin excessively red.

A clandestine Cabinet meeting was arranged behind the PM's back. Lord Godfrey Frogmore Levington was to be the new Philosopher King.

## Chapter 18

### DISASTER OR GREAT FORTUNE

"Gerry, my god, the headlines? Is this fake, or what?"

"Pass my glasses, Rodders, and do calm down, can't be…"

She glanced at the Times.

"A reliable source confirms that significant data has been lost for eternity. The country is digitally isolated due to the Doomsday virus. There is to be a complete British Revolution. Mortgages and other debts are wiped out, along with savings and pensions. The Government has sufficient resources to keep its people solvent during the metamorphosis of the political, social and economic landscape. This has been corroborated anonymously by sources close to the PM."

"Gerry, do you realise, our mortgage will be paid off? And those bloody credit cards we've been building up?"

"Pension's gone, but a lot of it went anyway, what with inflation and everything. It's a shock, Rodders, not sure how I feel. I mean, we didn't vote for this. How will everyone react? Will folks swallow this? Quick, turn on the latest news."

"This is the BBC. There has been rejoicing in the streets as the majority of struggling households are overnight freed of debt. There is an atmosphere of celebration and hope, with people sporting banners saying 'Levington levels up' and even 'Levington levitates'. There are, however, a small minority of protesters outside Parliament Square. Our reporter, Mike Jarvis, is at the scene. Mike…"

"Thank you, Pamela. As you can see, there are a number of well-known and less well-known faces here. Russian oligarchs, celebrities, influencers, company directors, you will hear them chanting in tune with their banners,

'Government Theft of our Money', 'This is Criminal' and 'We will fight in our Prada, we will fight in vintage Yves St Laurent, we will give you Dior but we will never surrender.' You will see, Pamela, the mood here is defiant and determined, mirroring their choreographed march and carefully planned attire, each protestor's outfit having at least something to do with the others, but clearly the overwhelming bullet is Prada."

"Thank you, Mike. We will bring you more updates throughout the day. This is Pamela Bucklesfield, BBC News."

Chapter 19

REALITY AND PERCEPTION

Gunnhilda and Loki were indeed entertained.

"Why didn't they believe me, Dad?"

"Well, my daughter, it's like this. Perceptions are unique to us all, Gods and humans alike. Eros is clouded by love, Foresti by justice,

Caishen by numbers, me by humour, you by over-attachment, and for them, well, some look at their world holistically, some in awe, some cannot see beyond the realms of a tiny bubble. Then their own perceptions can be manipulated. They suffer the indignity of falling prey to false perceptions, fake news, false digital profiles, commercially or religiously engineered contortions of reason."


Josh, Jenny and Phoebe held their precious gifts. The amber shone in the sunlight. Suddenly they saw the moving atoms, slowly coalescing into an image, it was a smiling Gunnhilda.

"You see her, Josh, Phoebe?"

"Yes Jenny" they said in unison.

"Mum, Dad, quick, look."

Sans glasses the image was clear to Geraldine, and Rodney rubbed his eyes, he looked, he saw…

"Unbelievable."

"She's fading."

"Must be some kind of collective, distorted perception, don't you think, Gerry?"

"Not so sure, Rodders. Not sure about anything anymore."

"Large G and no T?"

"Positive!"